FOOTBALL FUMBLINA

WRITTEN BY
MELICA NICCOLE

INSPIRED BY
ARIMA IMABOYA

ILLUSTRATED BY
VIVIANA MOYANO

PUBLISHED IN 2021
BY MELICA NICCOLE
AND HAMPTON PUBLISHING HOUSE, LLC

Football

Fumblina

Could have been

a ballerina.

Hung up her

ballet shoes.

To run some plays

and pay her dues.

Unbeknownst
to her
was risk.

Blue flags flying
tssk-tssk-tssk.

Fumble, Fumble,

Fumble, Fumble,

FOOTBALL

TOUCHDOWN VS FIELD GOAL

A TOUCHDOWN IS WHEN A TEAM SCORES POINTS BY RUNNING, PASSING, AND/OR CATCHING THE FOOTBALL ACROSS THEIR DESIGNATED SCORING AREA. A TOUCHDOWN IS WORTH 6 POINTS.

A FIELD GOAL IS THE PROCESS OF KICKING THE BALL BETWEEN THE GOAL POST. A FIELD GOAL IS WORTH 1 POINT OR 3 POINTS. IF A TOUCHDOWN IS MADE BEFORE THE FIELD GOAL THEN IT'S WORTH 1 POINT AND THREE POINTS WITHOUT A TOUCHDOWN.

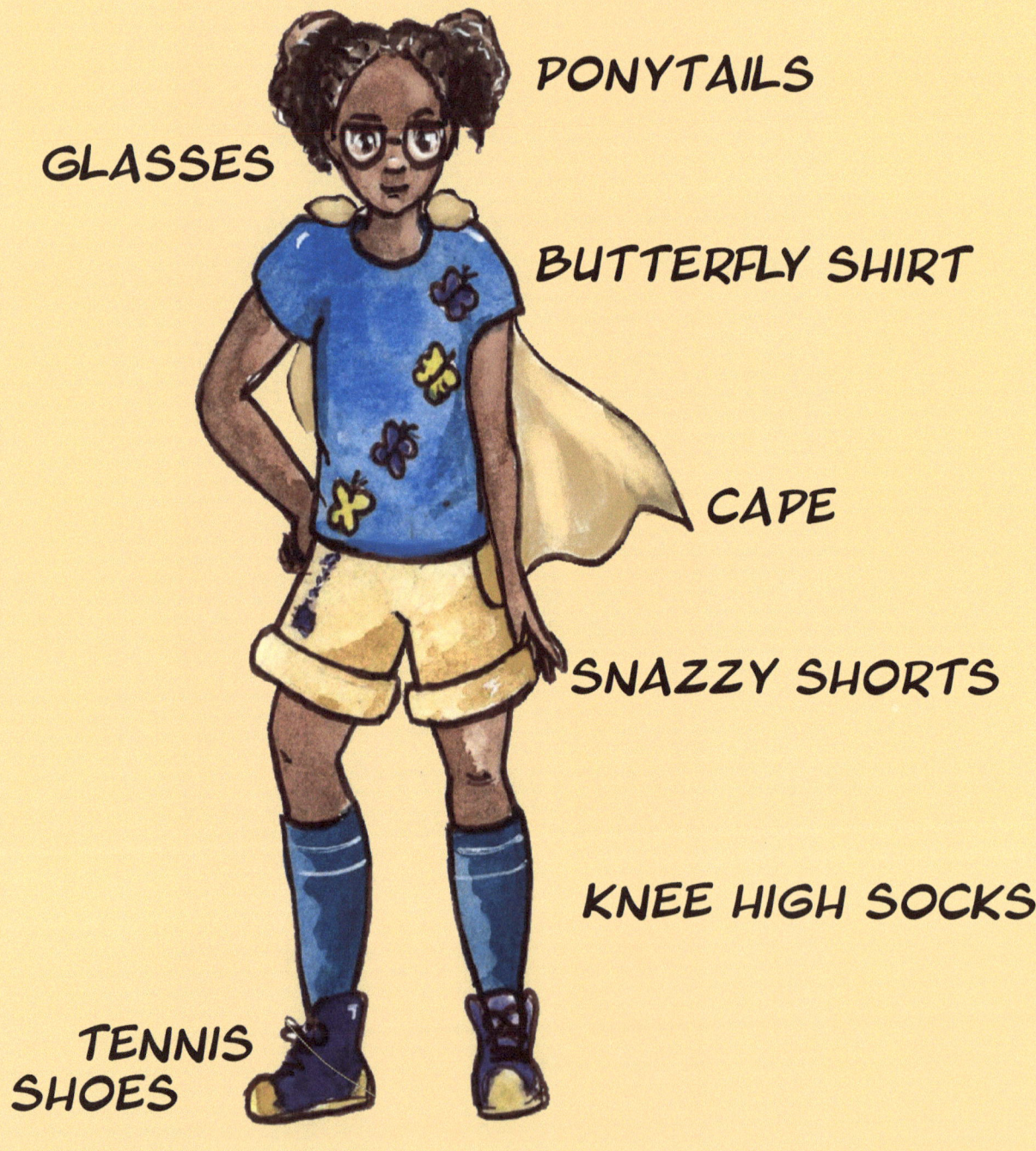

FOOTBALL FASHIONISTA

PONYTAILS

GLASSES

BUTTERFLY SHIRT

CAPE

SNAZZY SHORTS

KNEE HIGH SOCKS

TENNIS SHOES

FOOTBALL FASHIONISTA

PONYTAILS

GLASSES

FASHION JERSEY

FOOTBALL

FOOTBALL PANTS

HELMET

KNEE HIGH SOCKS

CLEATS

MILSON MERMER

BORN: COLUMBUS, OHIO

AGE: 33 YEARS OLD

JERSEY#: 2

POSITION: QUARTERBACK

TEAM: THE OHIO BUCKNEERS

2021 STATS

YARDS: 1195

TOUCHDOWNS: 11

INTERSECTION: 1

RATING: 125.3

HELMET PROTECTS YOU
FROM HARM THAT MAY COME YOUR WAY
BE SURE TO USE IT

HELMET

CLEATS

CLEATS
FOR YOUR FEET
RUN FASTER
THE FOOTBALL TACKLING MASTER
RUN FOR IT
RUN FOR IT
BEAT THE HEAT
RUN FOR IT
RUN FOR IT
WITH YOUR CLEATS

BEAUTIFUL GLASSES
HELP YOU SEE THINGS NEAR AND FAR
DURING FOOTBALL SEASON

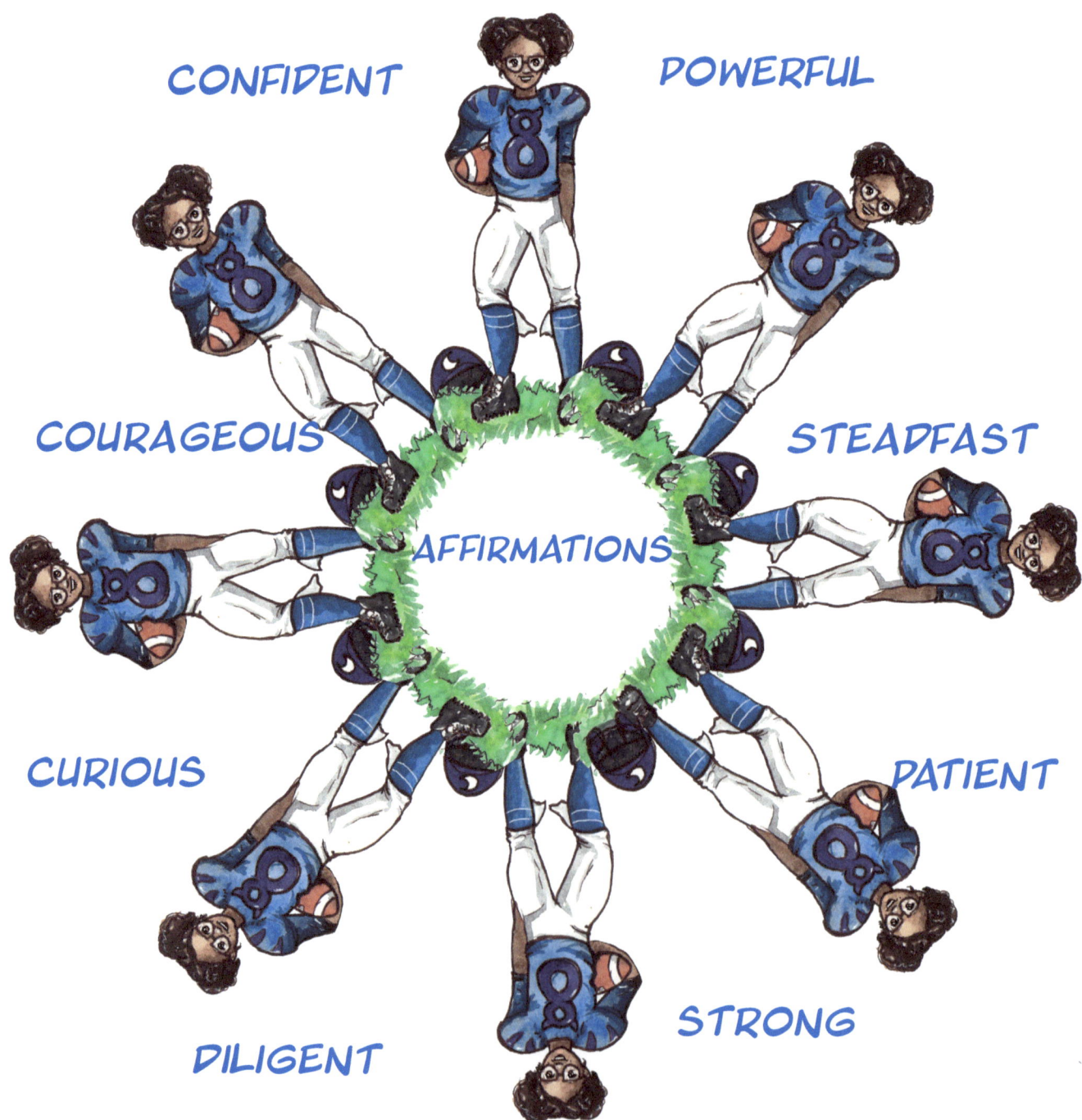

CONFIDENT

POWERFUL

COURAGEOUS

STEADFAST

CURIOUS

AFFIRMATIONS

PATIENT

DILIGENT

STRONG

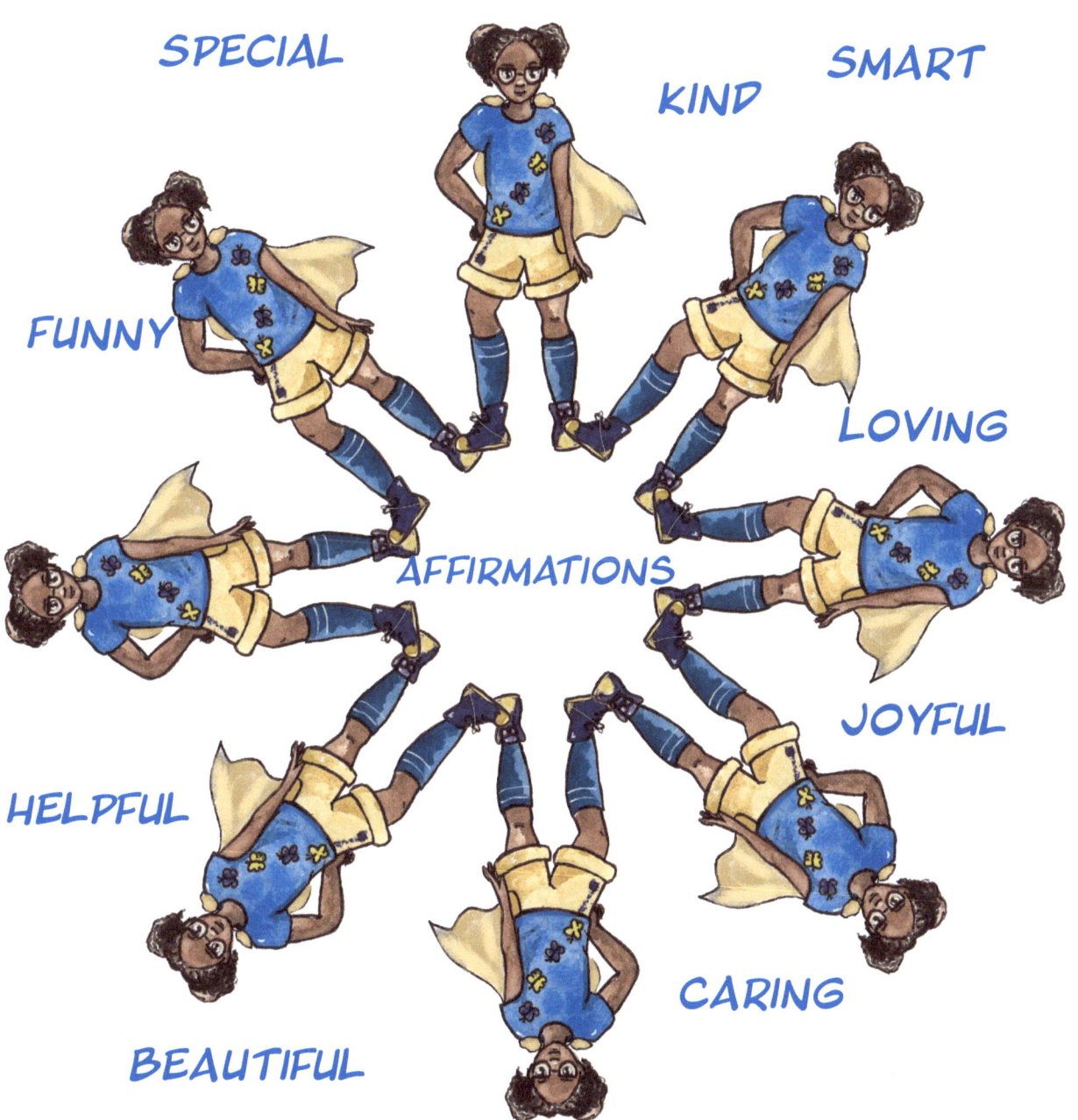

SPECIAL

KIND

SMART

FUNNY

LOVING

AFFIRMATIONS

HELPFUL

JOYFUL

BEAUTIFUL

CARING

THANK YOU FOR READING

CHECK OUT MY OTHER BOOKS ON
AMAZON.COM, BARNES AND NOBLE,
APPLE BOOKS, AND SMASHWORDS.

CHECK YOUR LOCAL BOOKSTORE FOR
TITLES AS WELL.

FOLLOW ME AT
MELICANICCOLE.COM
INSTAGRAM/MELICANICCOLE
TWITTER.COM/MELICANICCOLE

www.ingramcontent.com/pod-product-compliance
Lightning Source LLC
Chambersburg PA
CBHW041003170626
46815CB00002B/130